A mysterious laugh echoed across the field. All the players on the soccer field had noticed the noise and were looking around to see what was happening.

Then a strange, shivery voice echoed over the field: "*General Santiago! General Santiago!*" it shrieked.

Bryan felt a shiver begin at his toes and travel up his spine. He didn't believe in ghosts—but if he did, he was sure that was exactly what they would sound like.

"Oh, no," Sam called. "Look!"

Bryan gasped. At the opposite end of the field, a large white shape was drifting along in front of the goal. One of the players downfield screamed. Others watched, dumbstruck. Bryan squinted. His skin went cold. From a distance the shape appeared to be a life-size human skeleton!

Look for these other
Sports Mysteries books:

#1 The Case of the Missing Pitcher

#3 The Mystery of the Stolen Football

THE HAUNTED SOCCER FIELD

T.J. EDWARDS

ILLUSTRATED BY CHARLES TANG

SCHOLASTIC INC.
New York Toronto London Auckland Sydney

ISBN 0-590-48453-2

Produced by Daniel Weiss Associates, Inc.
33 West 17th Street, New York, NY 10011

12 11 10 9 8 7 6 5 5 6 7 8 9/9 0/0

Printed in the U.S.A. 40

First Scholastic printing, July 1995

To Madeleine

THE HAUNTED SOCCER FIELD

General Santiago

Bryan O'Malley felt like the luckiest kid in the world. He adjusted his goalie gloves and glanced around at the huge stadium. The stands reached up toward the clear Minnesota sky. The soccer field stretched away in front of him. It was hard to believe that he and his team, the Smithfield Sonics, were actually playing in a real stadium—the same stadium that one of the top professional teams from Brazil would be using over the next couple of days for a series of exhibition games.

"Hey, space cadet, quit daydreaming," yelled Sam Jansen, the Sonics' center defenseman. "We've got a game to win here!"

Bryan pushed a lock of red hair out of his eyes and grinned at Sam. "What are you worried about? This game's in the bag," he called. There was one minute left in their quarterfinal match against the Bolton Badgers. The Sonics were up by one goal, and the ball was at the other end of the field.

"It's looking good, all right," Sam said. "But don't forget that in 1994 Romania lost to Sweden in the quarterfinals on last-minute penalty kicks."

Bryan smiled. Sam was a walking encyclopedia of sports history. He knew everything from Willie Mays's batting average in 1954 to Larry Bird's lifetime free-throw shooting percentage.

As the final seconds ticked away, Bryan was already thinking about the semifinals of the Ridgefield County

Junior Tournament scheduled for the next afternoon. If the Sonics won that game, they would play for the championship. Bryan could picture it. The stadium would be jam-packed. The Sonics would play an amazing game, winning it all in the final seconds. He and his teammates would be heroes. They would be taken to city hall in a long white limousine. The mayor would come out to greet them and give them the key to the city. . . .

"Hey, Bryan! *Bryan!*"

Bryan looked up. "What . . . ?"

Suddenly a pack of Badgers was sprinting toward him! Danny Glencoe, the Badgers' star forward, was weaving through the Sonics with the ball.

How in the world had this happened? Where were his teammates? Just a few seconds ago the Sonics had been in total control!

Bryan watched helplessly as Danny dribbled left, then right. Sam made a move, rushing toward Danny from the left, but Danny quickly passed the ball to a teammate on his right. Sam lunged after the ball, but the Badger player passed it back to Danny, who took the ball straight for the goal.

Bryan's heart was thumping. He leaned forward on his toes, ready to spring.

Danny was twenty feet away. . . .

Fifteen . . .

Ten . . .

Bryan tensed for the shot—*Boom!*

The ball rocketed toward the lower right corner of the net. Bryan dove, stretching out his arms . . . and missed!

The crowd rose to its feet and roared, almost drowning out the sound of the buzzer ending the second half. *Tie game!*

Bryan couldn't bear to even lift his face from the dirt. He pounded his fists into the ground. If only he had gotten his hands on the ball! If only he had been paying closer attention!

Now there would be an overtime period. Anything could happen in overtime—

Bryan felt as if he had just cost the Sonics their chance at the championship.

"Hey," a familiar voice called. "Get up!"

Bryan slowly lifted his head and peered over his shoulder. Sam was leaning against the goalpost.

"I messed up," Bryan muttered. "I messed up big."

"Yeah," Sam replied, "but you were lucky."

Bryan squinted at his friend. "Lucky? What do you mean?"

Just then Lara Martini jogged over and playfully nudged Bryan with her foot. Besides being the Sonics' center halfback, Lara was known around Jefferson Elementary for reading two detective novels a week. "Boy, are you lucky, Bryan! I can't believe that shot hit the goalpost."

Bryan's eyes went wide, and he sat up. "It did? Are you kidding?" He looked toward the center of the field, where the rest of his team was . . . celebrating!?

"See?" Lara said, smiling. "We won!"

"Wow. We *did* luck out this time," he

said, letting Sam help him up. "Hey, what are we waiting for? Let's join the party!"

The three friends jogged to midfield, where the rest of their teammates were shaking hands with the Badgers.

A balding man holding a calculator came bustling toward them. It was Mr. Lester, a full-time accountant and the Sonics' coach.

"Wonderful!" Mr. Lester cried, punching numbers into his calculator. "The odds of the final shot of a game hitting the goalpost are at least a thousand to one. Well done!"

Bryan smiled. "Thanks, Mr. Lester."

"Tomorrow we play the Wolverines in the semifinals," Mr. Lester went on, taking a sheet of graph paper out of his pocket. "Hmmm . . . according to my statistics their goal-per-game average has been down over the last five contests. We're in good shape. And another thing—their average sneaker size is on par with . . ."

Before Mr. Lester could finish, Jack

Cummings and Corey Johnstone rushed up to them. Jack slapped Bryan hard on the back. "Real nice save," he said with a smirk. "Good thing you had that goalpost to help you."

"Thanks, Jack," Bryan said, giving the smaller boy a friendly shove. "And thanks for letting the entire Badger team get in front of the goal with no defenders."

Jack shrugged. "Hey," he said, "I can't be everywhere at once, you know? I'm only human."

"That's right," Lara said. "We can't all be Corey."

Corey Johnstone was the Sonics' star forward, and one of the fastest fifth graders in the county. She was slim, with black curly hair, and was the best soccer player on the team. She had scored two of the Sonics' three goals. "Hey, so I happen to like soccer," she said.

"Lucky for us you do," Sam said. "Especially if it helps us win the championship."

Corey, Sam, Bryan, Lara, and Jack had been through many sports battles together as best friends and teammates on the Sonics, the Smithfield Community Center's team. They had played baseball, football, and basketball against other teams of ten- and eleven-year-olds in the Ridgefield County Athletic League.

The five friends headed toward the locker room. "Don't forget, we still have to beat the Wolverines tomorrow before we make it to the finals," Bryan said.

"Don't worry. We will," Corey said confidently. "What I want is to beat the pants off the Hornets for the championship!"

The others nodded. The Johnsonville Hornets were their archrivals in every sport from baseball to basketball.

Lara glanced down and began to laugh. "It sure looks like Jack is confident about tomorrow's game," she said. "He's even found something to read in case he gets bored." She pointed to Jack's foot. A piece of newspaper was stuck to the bottom of his cleats.

Jack lifted his foot and grabbed the flapping piece of paper. "Very funny," he said, starting to crumple it.

"Hold on a minute," Lara said. "Not so fast."

"Why?" Jack asked. "I know you like to read, Lara, but . . ."

"Well, this looks pretty interesting," Lara replied. She took the newspaper page and smoothed it out. A headline printed in block letters across the top read: GENERAL SANTIAGO'S STOLEN MEDALLION MAY BE IN RIDGEFIELD.

"General who?" Bryan asked. "Never heard of him."

"Neither have I," Lara said. "But it sounds like a mystery." She cleared her throat and read aloud.

> "Brazilian authorities report that the grave of General Manuel Santiago was robbed one month ago. Santiago, a Brazilian war hero from the nineteenth century, was buried

RIDGEFIELD TIMES
Priceless Stolen Medallion Tracked to Ridgefield"
Sonics

with a host of jewels and trinkets, the most valuable of which was a gold medallion with an engraving of a warrior marching off to battle. The medallion had been in Santiago's family for over five hundred years."

"Five hundred years!" Bryan said with a whistle. "That's a long time."

Lara nodded, then continued to read.

"Authorities believe that twelve rings and the medallion, which is rumored to be cursed, may be in Ridgefield County. Before he died, General Santiago declared that if the medallion was ever taken from his grave, everyone near it would be haunted by his ghost until it was returned."

Lara looked up from the paper.

"Wow," Jack exclaimed. "A ghost!"

"How in the world would a cursed

medallion get all the way up here from Brazil?" Corey wondered.

Lara skimmed the rest of the article. "It says that the police suspect the crooks are part of a larger smuggling ring and are looking to sell it to someone in Canada," she said.

"Well, I'm going to be on the lookout for ghosts, that's for sure," Bryan commented.

"BOO!"

The five friends jumped. Standing behind them, laughing hysterically, were two fourteen-year-olds, Gus Cranston and Wayne Shorter. They were fixtures at the Smithfield Community Center, usually causing some sort of trouble.

"Ha, ha! Scared you little kids!" Gus cried. He was wearing a red T-shirt, yellow shorts, and green sneakers. Bryan thought he looked like a chubby stoplight.

"Oooooooo," Wayne howled. "A ghost is coming to get you!"

"Aw, bug off, you beanpole!" Bryan exclaimed. Wayne was as tall and thin as Gus was short and chubby. "We never said we believe in ghosts."

"Sure you don't," Gus replied. "I bet each one of you has to sleep with Mommy and Daddy tonight."

"You mean like you've done every night of your life?" Jack replied, puffing out his chest.

"Very funny, little man," Wayne said, stepping forward. Jack came up to his chest. "We'll just see who's scared when General Santiago's ghost comes around."

Laughing wildly, the two boys walked away.

"What a couple of jerks," Sam muttered.

"I should have let them have it!" Jack declared. "Wrestled them down and dragged their faces in the mud!" He punched an imaginary opponent.

"Hey, check it out!" Corey interrupted. She pointed toward the field, where two men in orange uniforms were passing a soccer ball expertly back and forth. Their feet moved so quickly it was hard to follow the motions.

"They're excellent!" Sam said. "They must be from the Brazilian team. I can't wait to see their exhibition match."

Jack nodded. "Check out that footwork."

Suddenly Bryan noticed that Corey was grinning, looking very pleased with herself. "What is it?" Bryan asked.

"How would you guys like to visit the Brazilian team locker room?" Corey said casually.

"Sure," Jack said sarcastically. "And right after that, we'll fly to Chicago and pay a visit to the Bears and the Cubs."

"No joke," Corey said. "My dad is friends with the equipment manager, Felipe Lopes. Dad met Felipe on a business trip to Brazil years ago. Felipe came over for dinner last night. He promised to show me around today—and my friends, too, of course."

"Are you serious?" Bryan demanded. "You've known about this all day and you didn't tell us?"

"We're never going to speak to you again!" Jack said, jokingly.

"I wouldn't recommend that," Corey said. "If you don't speak to me, then you don't get to meet the Brazilian team. Now come on, let's go!"

The Gift

As the five friends entered the Brazilian team's locker room, a dark-haired young man with a friendly smile and a mole on his left cheek hurried forward to greet them. It was Felipe, the equipment manager. Corey introduced him to her friends.

"You kids played a fine game today—excellent!" Felipe said with only a slight accent. "I saw most of it from the stands." He winked at Bryan. "Got a little help from the goalpost, eh?"

Bryan blushed and shrugged. He was

too excited about being in a professional soccer team's locker room to mind being teased a little.

Felipe led the kids over to where the members of the team were preparing for practice. At one end of a long bench a slim, dark-skinned man sat checking the bandages on his ankle, which was propped up on a chair. He held a bag of ice in one hand. Felipe introduced the injured man as Paulo Alvares, the star of the team.

"Hi." Paulo greeted the kids with a shy smile. "I'd get up to shake your hands, but I don't think it would be a good idea right now."

The kids laughed.

"Did you hurt your ankle during a game?" Bryan asked.

Paulo blushed. "I wish I could say so, but I really only tripped getting out of my car." He shook his head. "Bad luck."

"Bad luck? Bad luck? You let me tell you about bad luck!" a voice boomed.

The gang looked up to see a powerfully built man with a thick mustache stomp over.

"What's wrong now, Jorge?" asked Felipe. The kids recognized the newcomer as Jorge Pinzón, the Brazilian team's head coach. His picture had been in the local paper the week before.

"Bad luck is all we've had since this trip began," Jorge moaned. "It's bad enough we have to travel so much on this tour, but the Brazilian Soccer Association wouldn't even give us enough money to cover expenses! You know where I have to be tomorrow afternoon? At a fund-raising lunch at the Ridgefield County Athletic League!"

Paulo chuckled softly. "That Jorge," he said as the coach stomped away. "Always complaining about something."

Felipe laughed. "I'd better go check the equipment before the match, or he'll really have something to complain about," he said, heading for a door on one side of the room.

Just then a young woman whisked into the room through the door on the other side. "I hope everyone's dressed, 'cause here I come!" she sang out. Then she spotted the visitors. "Hey, you're the kids who just played, right?" she exclaimed.

"Yes," Bryan said. "We're all members of the Smithfield Sonics."

"Betsy Rodrigues. I'm the team's travel and finance coordinator. I book all the air flights and hotels and manage all the money. All the little bits and pieces."

"And you sure don't do it cheap enough!" Jorge bellowed from the other side of the locker room.

The woman ignored him. She sat down on the bench next to Paulo, pulled a small bottle of orange nail polish out of her pocket, and began to touch up her fingernails. "You know, you kids were really terrific today," she said. She winked at Corey. "Especially you, my friend. You could run circles around these Brazilian boys."

Corey grinned. "I doubt it. But thanks."

Suddenly Betsy stopped painting her nails and turned to Paulo. "Hey, I just had a great idea. We should give these kids a prize for their win today!"

"Sure," Paulo said agreeably. "They deserve it."

"That really isn't necessary—" Sam began.

"Nonsense," Betsy interrupted, waving her fingernails dry. "I've got just the thing. Don't move."

Moments later, Betsy bustled back into the room carrying a soccer ball. "Here you are, kids," she said, handing the ball to Corey. "In honor of your big win."

"Wow!" Corey said. "I don't know what to say."

"Say nothing," Betsy said. "Enjoy it! A gift from South America."

"But . . ." Lara began.

"No buts," Betsy said, standing up. "It is a gift from us to you."

"Right," Paulo said. "You have a game

tomorrow? Use it! Maybe it'll bring you good luck." He shook his head. "Not like the bad luck we've been having," he added softly.

"What's all this talk about bad luck?" Lara asked, taking the ball from Corey and tossing it in the air. She lobbed the ball back to Corey.

"Pay no attention to him," Betsy said, frowning at Paulo. "He is much too superstitious."

Lara opened her mouth to ask another question, but she was interrupted by Jorge.

"What in the world are you doing?" he cried, rushing over. "Betsy, don't tell me you're giving away one of our good game balls. This team is broke enough as it is!"

"Oh, calm down, Jorge," Betsy said. "Stop being such a miser. The kids played a good game today, and they deserve a little gift."

"And you couldn't give them an old

ball?" Jorge cried. "It had to be one of the new ones?"

Betsy shook her head. "It wouldn't be the same."

Jorge glanced at the kids and shrugged. "What good is it arguing?" he said. "Betsy always gets her way." He turned away with a scowl.

Betsy winked at the kids. "You'd better get going before the old grump changes his mind," she said. "Go on! Thanks for the visit. And I hope you'll be cheering us on at all our matches."

"We sure will," Sam promised for all of them.

The five friends turned to go. But at that moment there was a commotion in the locker-room entryway. Three police officers strutted into the room, followed by a dark-haired man in a trench coat. He twirled an unlit cigarette in his right hand.

"Well, well, well," the man in the trench coat said, looking around. "Commence the search!"

"Search for what?" Betsy asked. "Who are you?"

The dark-haired man chuckled. "You obviously aren't from these parts, madam." He cleared his throat and looked around at the Brazilian team members, who had all gathered to see what was going on. "I must confess to being somewhat of a, shall we say, public figure. You are looking at the man who single-handedly cracked the Minkstone Sausage Caper. I am Detective Morton Peck of the Smithfield Police."

Lara's eyes widened. A real police detective had come to search the locker room.

"But what are you searching for?" Betsy asked Detective Peck.

"I know," Paulo said with a laugh. "He's looking for all the goals we've ever missed!"

"Quite amusing," the detective said, frowning, "but this is no joke, I'm afraid. I'm searching for General Santiago's missing medallion!"

Paulo's eyes widened. "The haunted medallion? You think it might be here in our locker room?"

Detective Peck nodded. "I have reason to suspect so."

Everyone in the room began to chatter excitedly, and Jorge stepped forward. "Let me see your search warrant, please. My players don't need this bother."

"Fair enough," Detective Peck said. He reached into his trench-coat pockets and began to pull out assorted scraps of paper. "Ah . . . I know it's here somewhere. Hold on, now. Yes, here it is. . . . No, no—that's my laundry bill. Ten dollars for my shirts—highway robbery! Oh, here we go." He held up a crumpled piece of paper.

Jorge reached for it. The coach narrowed his eyes as he read. Then he sighed. "Well, go ahead and search, then. But be quick."

The three officers began to make a thorough search of the locker room.

"It's the curse of the medallion," Paulo

said. "I know it is. It's the only explanation for all our bad luck."

"Then you believe the legend?" Jack asked. "You think General Santiago will haunt whoever takes the medallion?"

Paulo nodded solemnly. "You can laugh if you want. But I know the legend is true. The general won't rest in peace until his medallion is recovered. If he thinks it's here, the team will keep having bad luck until it's found." He gestured at his bandaged ankle. "Isn't that the proof? It's the ghost that made me sprain my ankle."

"Oh, stop whining," Betsy said. "Your ankle will be all right. And don't blame ghosts just because you're clumsy."

"Why do the police think the medallion is here, anyway?" Lara wondered.

Paulo shrugged. "That's a good question. Maybe someone gave them a tip."

"Maybe," Betsy said. "But who? We're a soccer team, not a gang of thieves."

Detective Peck wandered over just in

time to hear her comment. "Thieves can hide in strange places. I once found a gang of robbers living in a pickle factory."

"Wow," Bryan said. "What'd you do?"

Detective Peck raised a single eyebrow. "What did I do? I gave them a shower and sent them to jail."

The police searched every inch of the place. "Nothing here, boss," one of the officers told Detective Peck.

The detective frowned and glanced around. "Before we leave we'll want to search everyone here," he announced.

"Come on, let's get out of here," Lara whispered to the others. "The police obviously aren't getting anywhere with this case. Maybe we should open our own investigation."

"That's a great idea," Corey agreed. "We'll figure out where that medallion is, ghost or no ghost."

They all nodded and headed for the door. But before they reached it, the detective strode across the room.

"Trying for a quick getaway, are you, kids?" he said. "I'm afraid we'll have to search you before you go."

"What?" Jack exclaimed. "Search us?"

"I'm afraid so," Peck said. "I've seen some odd things in my day. I once found ten grand on a day-old baby. We wouldn't want one of you accidentally walking off with the medallion. Just raise your hands over your heads. This won't take long."

Peck quickly patted down the boys while a female police officer checked the girls. The only thing they found was Corey's track medal in her windbreaker pocket.

"They're clean," the policewoman said when she was through.

"Okay, kids," Peck said. "Sorry for the inconvenience."

With a final good-bye to the Brazilian team, the gang headed out the door.

"Wow!" Bryan said once they were outside. "I can't believe we all got frisked, just like in the movies!"

"It was kind of cool," Jack agreed. "Of

course, if he had arrested us, I would've knocked him flat."

"Sure," Sam said as Jack karate-chopped an imaginary policeman.

"Well, I wonder where that medallion is," Corey said, kicking their new soccer ball to Sam.

"Man, Corey," Sam said, chasing down the ball, "I'm only ten feet away. You don't have to give the ball any fancy spin."

"Sorry, Sam, I didn't even mean to."

"I think it'll be a cinch to find the medallion," Bryan said.

"Who are you—Sherlock Holmes?" Lara asked.

"No," Bryan replied. "But this case is simple. Just keep your eye out for the ghost of a dead general. Whoever he haunts is the crook. Now come on. We'd better get going, or we're all going to be late for dinner!"

The Ghostly Garage

"You'd better get over here quickly," Corey said to Lara on the phone early the next morning. "And bring the rest of the gang."

"What's the matter?"

"We had a break-in last night, and my little sister and I both heard ghosts!"

Bryan, Jack, Sam, and Corey were already gathered outside Corey's garage when Lara arrived.

"So what's the story?" Lara asked, skidding to a halt on her bike.

"It's just like I told you," Corey said. "Someone or something broke into my family's garage last night. I'm glad Gus and Wayne aren't around to hear this, but I was really scared. It sounded like a ghost was prowling around all last night."

"What do you mean?" Lara asked.

Corey bit her lip and glanced at her friends. "Well, it was just like in the movies. There was this strange otherworldly whistling."

"Wow!" Bryan said. "You think it was the ghost of General Santiago out for revenge?"

"I don't know," Corey replied shakily. "All I know is that nothing was taken, and the place is a mess." Corey led them into the garage.

"This *is* strange," Lara said, looking around. "Have you called the police?"

"They should be here anytime now."

"I'm just glad nothing happened to my new car!" exclaimed a muffled voice. Corey's father was bent over the engine of a brand-new blue sports car parked inside the garage.

"That's some car, Mr. Johnstone," Bryan said.

"Thanks, Bryan," Mr. Johnstone said, straightening up. "And you're right, it *is* some car. It's a finely tuned machine, capable of going from zero to sixty in three-point-five seconds. And just look at the interior. Top class all the way. Let me show you kids a thing or two about the engine."

Corey cleared her throat. "Uh, Dad, do you mind?"

Mr. Johnstone sighed. "I suppose you're right." He winked at Bryan. "I'll show you the motor later," he said, and headed inside.

Lara looked around. The Johnstones had a two-car garage, but they parked their station wagon on the street and used the extra space for storage. Tools were strewn everywhere. Bats, balls, mitts, and masks that were usually stored in a bin in the corner were scattered on the floor. Two gym bags were ripped open and thrown on top of a woodpile in the corner. Gym shorts, T-shirts, and sneakers lay all over the room, including a single white sock that dangled from a light fixture overhead.

Suddenly Lara gasped. "Look, guys," she exclaimed. "Our first clue." She pointed to an open window at the top of the back wall of the garage.

"So maybe it wasn't a ghost," Sam said. "A ghost wouldn't need an open window—he'd just breeze right through the wall!"

"And that whistling might have come from this window being open," Lara added. "A draft might have whistled in through the garage and into the house."

"I suppose it's possible," Corey said hesitantly.

"What time did you start hearing the whistling, Corey?"

"Let's see now. We parked the station wagon on the street, and walked in through the front door, and I went to go brush my teeth. That's when I first noticed it."

"So, assuming it was the window, it must have been open by the time you got home," Lara said.

"Right," Jack said. "And the crime must have been committed while you were all at dinner."

"Okay, we've narrowed down the time of the break-in," Lara said. "Maybe we can find more clues." She gestured to Bryan. "Give me a lift. I want to take a closer look at that window."

"No problem," Bryan replied. "But take it easy on my back, okay? Don't forget that I've got to play goal this afternoon."

The others smiled. The big semifinal game against the Wolverines was scheduled for one o'clock that afternoon. If they won, they would face their archrivals, the Hornets, that evening.

With some help from Corey and Sam, Lara climbed onto Bryan's shoulders.

Balancing carefully, she stuck her head out the window and looked out. She ran her hand over the windowsill. Everything seemed normal. Then she spotted something—a brown smudge in the middle of the sill. She looked closer, then gasped. The smudge looked a lot like dried blood!

"Okay, you can let me down," she called to Bryan. As soon as she was safely on the ground again, Lara told her friends what she had found.

"Are you sure it's blood?" Bryan asked, rubbing his shoulder.

Lara shrugged. "Of course I'm not sure," she said. "But what else could it be? Whoever broke in must have cut himself."

"Or herself," Jack put in.

"Or itself," Corey said. "Do ghosts bleed?"

"Great," Sam said. "So we're looking for a crook with a scratch. That really narrows things down."

"What I want to know," Lara asked,

"is how anyone got up to the window in the first place. It's eight feet off the ground."

"Good point," Bryan said. "Let's check outside."

Moments later the gang was outside, looking up at the open window.

"You'd have to be a giant to reach that high," Sam said.

"Or a ghost," Corey said.

"Or maybe just an adult," Bryan added. "A six-footer would only have to jump up two feet to grab the ledge."

Lara got down on her knees and examined the ground beneath the window. "Check this out," she said.

There in the dirt was a group of well-marked footprints.

"Someone's been here, all right," Bryan noted. "But I can't tell if all these prints were made by the same pair of shoes."

"Maybe there was more than one robber," Lara said. "Either way, these footprints are dug pretty deep into the dirt.

They must have jumped down from the window to the ground."

"Yeah," Jack said. "And I don't see any ladder marks, so they must have pulled themselves up through the window."

Lara stood back up. "Okay, so we're looking for a tall guy. . . ."

"Or two maybe not-so-tall people," Jack said.

"Or a great jumper," Bryan added.

"Or a ghost," Corey said. "I'm still not convinced that what I heard was the wind."

"But why would a ghost haunt you?" Sam asked. "You don't have the medallion, do you?"

"Of course not," Corey said. "But don't you remember what the newspaper said? The ghost promised to haunt everyone anywhere near the medallion, not just the person who stole it. It might mean that the medallion is somewhere nearby."

Lara looked skeptical. But before she could reply, there was a wrenching cry from inside the garage.

"ARRRGHHH!"

The gang's skin froze.

Corey gasped. "That's my dad!" she cried, running for the garage door.

Mr. Johnstone was bent over his blue sports car.

"My car!" he wailed. "My beautiful, beautiful car!"

"What's wrong?" Sam asked. "It looks okay to me."

"Looks okay?" Mr. Johnstone cried. "Take a closer look, my boy."

The gang gathered around the hood and looked where he was pointing. "What is it?" Jack asked, squinting. "I see a little smudge there, but—"

"A smudge?" Mr. Johnstone thundered. "It's more than a smudge. It's a mark—a bright orange mark! Someone has ruined the finish on my new car."

At that moment a police car pulled into the driveway. Two officers climbed out. "We had a call about a break-in at this address," said one of them.

"That's right, Officer," Mr. Johnstone said. "But I've just discovered that it wasn't just a break-in. There's vandalism involved as well." He gestured dramatically at his car. "Look! An orange smudge mark on the hood!"

The officer raised her eyebrows. "I'm sure it'll rub right off, sir. Now, why don't you tell us about the break-in." She pulled a notebook out of her back pocket. Corey and her father told her what had happened, while the second officer took a look around the garage.

When the Johnstones had finished, the first officer nodded. "It seems you were lucky. If you do discover anything missing later, give me a call. In the meantime, I'll file a report." She snapped her notebook shut. Then she and her partner got into their car and drove away.

Mr. Johnstone turned to the kids. "Well, that's that," he said with a sigh. "They'll probably never catch the vandals who damaged my beautiful car." He glanced at his watch. “Hey, don’t you kids have a game today? You’d better get changed.”

In all the excitement they had almost forgotten about the big semifinal game.

“We’d better get a move on,” Jack exclaimed as Mr. Johnstone went inside. “This mystery-solving and ghost-hunting will have to wait. We’ve got a game to win!”

A Ghostly Game

"The key to any athletic competition is preparation," Mr. Lester said in his pre-game pep talk. "My studies show me that the most prepared team wins big games over seventy percent of the time." Mr. Lester pointed to his calculator to emphasize his point.

"That's part of why the Oakland A's did so well in the late 1980s," Sam put in. "Their manager, Tony La Russa, is among the best prepared in the business."

"Excellent point, Sam!" Mr. Lester

exclaimed. "Talent alone only takes a squad so far. Now, my statistical analysis of every World Cup soccer match dating back to 1954 tells me that the team that scores first wins the match over sixty percent of the time. So I urge you to take lots of shots on goal. Go get 'em, Sonics!"

Bryan positioned himself at goal and let Sam take practice shots. Meanwhile, Corey stretched at midfield; Jack, the right wing, jogged in place; and Lara was warming up with some jumping jacks.

"We're gonna win big," Sam cried, pounding the ball at Bryan. "I can feel it! We're like the 1927 Yankees. Or the Celtics in the early 1960's. They won eight NBA titles in a row."

Bryan dove to his left and caught the ball. Out of the corner of his eye he saw Felipe walking toward the offices at the back of the stadium.

"Hey!" he called. "Felipe!"

But the Brazilian kept walking without looking around.

“Felipe!” Bryan shouted again.

“He must not be able to hear you,” Sam said. “Come on. Let me take a few more shots.”

Just then a voice crackled over the PA system.

“Welcome to Ridgefield Stadium for the Ridgefield County Junior Tournament semifinal match between the Smithfield Sonics and Westerly Wolverines!”

The small crowd cheered as the referee clapped his hands for attention. “Team captains, front and center,” he called.

Corey jogged over to join the ref. So did Ricky Harling, a tall boy who was known throughout the league for being a terrific ball handler.

“All right,” the ref said. “You all know the rules. Two half-hour halves. One sudden-death overtime period, if needed. The Wolverines have won the coin toss, so it’s their ball. Let’s play!”

The two teams took position and a whistle blew. Ricky Harling kicked the ball over the center line to his left forward. Jack attacked, but the boy quickly passed back to Ricky. Corey challenged him for the ball, but Ricky deftly dribbled the ball to his right, leaving Corey in the dust.

"Wow," Bryan thought, getting ready for some serious action. "That guy is good!" He knew there wouldn't be any room for mistakes against this team. He couldn't count on the goalpost to help him out again.

Ricky dribbled upfield, then passed the ball to a teammate racing down the field on his right. Sam ran to intercept, but a second later the ball was soaring back to Ricky, who took the pass with his chest and continued dribbling toward the goal. Lara came sprinting over to help out. But Ricky was fast—the next thing anyone knew, he had scooted around another Sonic player and was facing Bryan for a shot on goal.

Heart pounding, Bryan leaned forward,

ready to jump. Ricky faked to his right. Bryan kept his eye on the ball. Ricky faked to his left. Bryan flinched and, off balance, watched helplessly as Ricky pounded the ball behind him into the net.

"Goal!" the announcer cried.

Bryan slammed his fists into the ground. The Wolverines mobbed Ricky. On the sidelines, Bryan could see Mr. Lester frantically punching numbers into his calculator.

"Don't worry!" he called to Bryan. "Teams sometimes come from behind. The odds are stacked against you, but you can do it. Besides, teams with red-headed goalies always win!"

"Is that true?" someone called from the stands.

Mr. Lester looked over his shoulder and shrugged. "Well, I actually don't have any numbers to back it up . . . but I try to be encouraging. . . ."

The ref retrieved the ball from the goal while the Sonics conferred.

"I think I'll lie back a bit when Ricky has the ball," Corey said. "He's really good."

"Good idea," Lara said. "Now let's get this goal back."

But that turned out to be easier said than done. The rest of the first half ticked away, and the Sonics only managed to take two shots on goal. Luckily, the Wolverines did no better: only four shots, two wide and two saved by Bryan.

"We've got to get more offense," Bryan said during halftime.

"My thoughts exactly," Mr. Lester said. "Now, listen up, team! The statistical probability of . . ."

The coach's numerical pep talk lasted right up to the buzzer for the second half. Then the Sonics headed back onto the field.

"Let's go, guys!" Bryan shouted, running to the goal. "Comeback time. Let's make this half something to remember!"

Unfortunately, the next twenty-five

minutes were decidedly forgettable. Neither team could generate any offense. Anytime the ball made it to the opposing area, it was kicked free before the team could get off a single shot. Corey, Jack, and the other Sonic offensive players couldn't shake loose from their defenders. With five minutes left to play, the score remained 1–0.

"I can't believe this," Bryan called to Sam when the ball was down at the other side of the field. "Why can't we score?"

Sam shrugged. Before he could answer, there was a funny crackling noise from the PA system.

The crackling grew louder. Then a mysterious laugh echoed across the field. By now everyone had noticed the noise and was looking around to see what was happening.

Then a strange, shivery voice echoed over the field: *"General Santiago! General Santiago!"* it shrieked.

Bryan felt a shiver begin at his toes

Sonics
Sonics

and travel up his spine. He didn't believe in ghosts—but if he did, he was sure that was exactly what they would sound like.

"Oh, no," Sam called. "Look!"

Bryan gasped. At the opposite end of the field, a large white shape was drifting along in front of the goal. One of the players downfield screamed. Others watched, dumbstruck. Bryan squinted. His skin went cold. From a distance the shape appeared to be a life-size human skeleton!

"What's it doing?" Sam asked.

"I don't know," Bryan said, his heart pounding.

The crowd was on its feet, confused and horrified. Bryan looked to the sidelines. Mr. Lester was nervously fiddling with his calculator as if computing would make the phantom disappear. Betsy and Felipe were looking on from just above in the stands.

A moment later, the phantom stopped short and howled. Then, before anyone could react, it glided for an exit and disappeared through it.

Here and there, nervous laughter erupted from the crowd. It sounded to Bryan as if people didn't know whether to think what had just happened had been scary or funny. On the field, all the players were talking at once.

The referee blew his whistle for order. "All right, enough practical jokes," he called out, looking disgusted. "We're trying to play ball here." He grabbed the ball from the ground and tossed it to Jack. "Let's go."

Bryan and Sam exchanged glances. "Do you—do you think it was a joke?" Sam asked.

"I'm not sure," Bryan said. He shook his head. "It looked like a ghost, it sounded like a ghost—who knows?"

Sam turned and saw that the ball was already back in play and headed their way. "Well, let's get the gang together and talk about it later," he said over his shoulder as he jogged back toward his position. "Real ghost or not, I bet it had something to do with that medallion!"

Bryan watched Sam race toward the action, slide-tackle a Wolverine who was just about to pass, and steal the ball. Sam immediately passed to Lara. She quickly dribbled up the field and crossed the ball to Jack, who was rushing up the other side of the field.

With one touch, Jack booted the ball to Corey just as she crossed the goalie box. Two Wolverines were quickly closing in, but Corey controlled the ball. As the first committed, she gave the ball a slight push with the outside of her right foot, dribbled around him, and blasted the ball toward the net.

Swat! The Wolverine goalie batted it down.

From the middle of a mob of players from both teams, Jack controlled the rebound and quickly shot again.

Swat! The Wolverine goalie batted it away.

Suddenly the ball rocketed into the Wolverine goal!

Bryan jumped in the air. "All right!" he cried.

"Yes!" Sam yelled at the same time.

"Who shot it?" Bryan called. "I couldn't tell from here."

"I don't know," Sam called back. "I couldn't see either."

But Ricky Harling's face told the story. The Wolverine star had accidentally scored a goal for the Sonics! As he ran back to help out, the ball had bounced off his foot straight into the net.

"Man!" he cried, kicking the ground as hard as he could.

"Shake it off, Ricky," a teammate said. "We'll get it back."

The Wolverine star had scored the only two goals of the day—one for each team!

"One to one," the ref called. "Three minutes to play."

The Wolverines had possession. Lara stole a sloppy pass but was immediately picked up by Ricky. From where Bryan was standing, he could tell that Lara, Jack, and Corey were doing everything they could. Lara passed to Jack, who cut right and squibbed the ball to Marla Armstrong, the Sonics' left halfback. He got it back a moment later and passed to Corey, who passed to Lara. But they just couldn't get past Ricky Harling and the rest of the Wolverines.

Ricky got a foot on a pass meant for Corey, and unintentionally booted the ball over his own team's end line.

"Corner kick!" the ref cried.

"Let Lara take it," Mr. Lester advised from the sidelines.

Lara hustled to the corner where the ref had placed the ball. The rest of the Sonics lined up in front of the Wolverine goal, and the Wolverines set up their defense.

"One minute remaining," the ref called.

Lara's heart was pounding. What a

day! First a break-in at Corey's garage, then a ghost on the field. And now a corner kick with a minute left to play.

Lara looked over the field. She could either try to go for a goal herself or else just put the ball in play right in front of the Wolverine goal.

With a deep breath, Lara took three steps, brought back her right foot, and sent the ball flying toward the middle of the field. Corey saw the ball coming and lay back. Players on both teams jostled for position.

Just as the ball came down, Corey cut around Ricky Harling, leaped high in the air, and headed the ball toward the left corner of the goal. Surprised, the Wolverine goalie dove for it, but the ball deflected off his fingertips into the net.

"Score!" the ref called.

The Sonics mobbed Corey.

"That's using your head!" Jack cried as the buzzer sounded. The game was over. The Sonics had won, 2–1.

For a few minutes there was pandemonium as the Sonics congratulated one another. Corey couldn't stop grinning as her teammates patted her on the head one by one. It had been a close game, and an exciting final minute. And best of all, the Sonics would be playing the Hornets in the championship game that evening!

Finally the team headed toward the locker room to change. Jack, Bryan, Corey, Sam, and Lara strolled off the field together. "Great game, everyone," Jack said once again.

Corey nodded. "I wonder if the ghost saw my great head shot," he commented.

Jack shuddered. "I can't believe I'm saying this, but that ghost looked awfully real to me," he said.

"Me too," Sam said. "I think this was the first time in the history of sports that a game was haunted."

Lara snorted. "I don't think so," she

said. "But *something* weird is going on, and I want to find out what it is."

"Right," Bryan said. "I say we get changed as fast as we can—then do some serious investigating!"

A SURPRISE IN THE SHED

"Where should we look first?" Jack asked a few minutes later. The stadium was emptying quickly.

"Why don't you and Corey check the announcer's booth," Lara suggested. She turned to Sam and Bryan. "We'll look over the grounds and see if we can find anything interesting."

"Okay," Sam said. "Let's hope ghosts leave trails."

While Jack and Corey headed for the announcer's booth, the others walked around the field, beginning with the area behind the Wolverines' goal where the ghost had appeared. Unfortunately, all they found were a few sets of footprints that *could* have been made by the ghost—or by one of the players.

After twenty minutes of searching, even Lara was ready to give up. Just then she saw Jack and Corey heading toward them.

"Did you guys find anything?" Corey called.

"Nope," Lara said. "What did the announcer say?"

"Just before the ghost appeared, someone called the announcer on the stadium phone and told him he was needed in the visiting locker room," Jack said. "As soon as he heard the strange sounds, he came running back, but by that time whoever was using the equipment was gone without a trace."

Sam sighed. "Well, we've got another game tonight. Could we call off the investigation for now? I've got to chill for a while."

"Good idea," Bryan said. "I'm going to stop by the supply shed and see if there's a spare ball I can borrow. I might practice a little this afternoon."

"You could use it," Jack mumbled.

Corey laughed. "We'll go with you, Bryan," she offered. "It's on the way out."

When they reached the small supply shed at the edge of the field, Bryan opened the door. "I'll be right out," he said, and disappeared inside.

He reappeared a moment later, looking excited. "Hey, you guys," he said. "Get in here. You have to see this."

Jack was the first one inside. "Whew!" he exclaimed. "It stinks in here. What is that, turpentine?"

"Never mind that," Bryan said, pointing. "Look!"

There on the floor were three soccer balls. They had been sliced open and their insides ripped out. A few cabinets had been ransacked, and towels and the contents of a first-aid kit were scattered about.

After an astonished pause, Sam spoke up. "Why would someone want to rip open three perfectly good soccer balls?" he wondered.

"Let's just think this through logically," Lara said. "There has to be some reason for doing this."

The gang was silent. A light breeze blew through the shed.

Suddenly Sam slapped his forehead. "We're such idiots!" he exclaimed. "Why does someone rip open a soccer ball? That's simple—to get something out of the inside."

Corey gasped. "Like a medallion!"

"Of course!" Lara exclaimed. "That explains everything. Someone must have smuggled the medallion out of South America in a soccer ball. And now they're trying to get it back."

"But why would people be cutting apart *these* soccer balls?" Sam asked. "Felipe keeps an eye on all the balls that would have come in from South America.

Wouldn't whoever hid the medallion know which ball it was in?"

"That," Lara said, her face falling, "is a good question."

Once again they all fell quiet. Then Corey let out a squeak.

"What is it?" Jack said.

"I'm about to be brilliant!" She looked around at her friends. "Don't you guys remember a little gift we were given yesterday?"

Lara snapped her fingers. "The soccer ball!"

"And Paulo and Betsy gave it to us just before the police came to look for the medallion," Jack cried, jumping up and down.

"And it was given to me!" Corey went on. "Maybe that's why my family's garage was broken into. The thief was looking for the ball."

Lara looked thoughtful. "Do you think we got the ball with the medallion in it by accident, or on purpose?"

"What do you mean?" Bryan asked.

"I mean, were we given that ball to get it out of the way while the police were around, or was it just by chance?"

"Well, let's think about it," Corey stated. "Who are the suspects if it was given to us on purpose?"

"There was Paulo, Jorge, Betsy, Felipe . . ." Bryan began.

"Not Felipe," Corey protested again. "He's my father's friend. He's not a thief."

"Probably not," Lara said. "But we've got to think of everyone."

"I think it was Jorge," Jack said. "He seemed pretty mean and he was always complaining about money."

"And don't forget Jorge didn't want us to take the ball away," Sam added. "He might not have wanted the medallion out of sight."

"And Betsy insisted that we take the ball she picked out for us even after Jorge asked her to give us an older one," Corey said.

"Gosh, it sounds like any one or all of them could all be in on it!" Bryan exclaimed, exasperated.

"Well, first things first," Sam said. "Let's be logical. I say we check out the soccer ball Betsy gave us. Do you still have it, Lara?"

"Sure," she said. "It's in my backyard."

"Then let's go find it, pronto," Bryan said. "General Santiago won't be able to rest until his medallion is back in his grave."

"And I sure wouldn't mind his ghost going with it," Corey said with a shudder.

A Surprise Arrest

Lara's little brother, Jimmy, came flying out of the house as the friends came up the walk.

"Hey, Lara! Come here quick!" he cried.

"Whoa, there," Lara said. "Slow down, Jimmy!"

"What is it, kid?" Bryan asked. "You look like you saw a ghost."

Jimmy's lower lip began to tremble, and he looked as though he might cry at any minute. "I did!"

Seconds later the gang was in Lara's

backyard. "Now tell us exactly what happened, Jimmy," Corey said gently.

Jimmy pointed to the swing set. "I was on the slide," he said. "And I got thirsty, so I went into the kitchen for a drink. I was about to go back outside when I saw a ghost come into the yard and take the soccer ball."

"Are you sure it was a ghost?" Lara asked. "Tell us what it looked like and what it did, okay?"

Jimmy whimpered a little and looked around, as if he feared the ghost would reappear at any moment. "It was a skeleton," he said at last.

The gang gasped.

"Wow!" Jack said. "That ghost travels fast!"

"How did the ghost get into the yard?" Lara asked her brother.

Jimmy shrugged. "I don't know. It was just like I told you. I had been playing with your new soccer ball . . ."

"I thought you said you were on the slide," Sam said.

The little boy nodded. "I was," he said, blushing and looking a little guilty.

"Jimmy," Lara said suspiciously. "Tell us the truth. What were you doing?"

"I *am* telling you the truth," Jimmy protested. He blushed again. "I was on the slide, and I had the soccer ball. . . . I was coloring."

Lara put her hands on her hips. "Let me get this straight. You were coloring on the soccer ball?"

Jimmy nodded. "With green crayon." He wrinkled his brow. "Was that wrong?"

"Don't worry about it," Lara said, rolling her eyes at her friends. "Tell us what happened with the ghost."

"Well, after I got my drink, I came back outside. That's when I saw him take the ball and run away."

"How long ago did all this happen?" Bryan asked.

"I don't know," Jimmy said. "Just a few minutes ago, I guess."

Lara glanced around. "Well, that ghost

is probably long gone by now."

"If the medallion was in the ball, at least we won't be haunted anymore," Corey pointed out.

"True," Lara said, "but if the ghost isn't a real ghost, I'd really like to know who was behind all this." She sighed. "I'm just not sure what we do next."

"Well," Sam said, "I guess we could check with costume stores and see if they have records of who bought skeleton costumes lately."

Corey shook her head. "How do we know when the costume was bought? Or where? That costume could have come from someone's garage—or from Brazil." She paused. "If it's a costume, that is, and not a real ghost."

"Right," Sam said, rolling his eyes. "Anyway, I say we pay a visit to the police. They probably have information we could use to crack the case."

A few minutes later the five friends

were busily stowing their bikes in the rack in front of the police station. They headed inside and immediately spotted Detective Peck talking to a fellow officer by the front desk. He was still wearing his trench coat.

"Ah, yes," he was saying as the kids entered. "The Pickle Factory Caper. Now, there was a crime scene. Myself, four of the most notorious criminals in Minnesota history, and twenty thousand bottled pickles. Most interesting. I've devoted an entire chapter of my memoirs to it. . . ."

"Excuse me, sir," Lara said politely, tapping the detective on the shoulder.

Detective Peck spun around and raised his eyebrows. "Well, if it isn't the gang of soccer-playing children."

"We have some information we thought might interest you," Lara said.

The detective listened carefully as Lara recounted the events of the day, beginning with the garage break-in and ending with the ghost.

"Very interesting," he said when she was through. "But you're a little late, I'm afraid. I've already cracked this case wide open."

"You have?" they all asked at once.

"Absolutely," Peck said. "Solved it even faster than the Smithfield Warehouse Caper. I already have a suspect in custody."

"Was he wearing a skeleton suit?" Sam asked in surprise.

"No," Peck replied. "He was dressed pretty normally. In fact, he was in the locker room when we searched yesterday. I believe you kids know him—Felipe Lopes."

The five friends looked at each other with disbelief.

"Felipe?" Corey said. "It can't be!"

"He's so nice," Jack said.

Peck nodded. "Sometimes the nicest people in the world are bad underneath," he said. "No. This one is in the bag, kiddies. We got a tip this morning. We went back to the locker room and found a key in Felipe's locker."

"A key to what?" Sam asked.

"A key to a locker at the Ridgefield bus station," Peck replied. "Inside the locker were the twelve rings that had been stolen from the grave. The only thing missing was General Santiago's medallion," he said with a frown. He narrowed his eyes. "But I'll find that, too, just mark my words," he added quickly.

The gang was dumbfounded. Only Lara was still thinking. "When did you arrest Felipe?" she asked the detective.

"I'd say around two-thirty," Peck replied.

"But my little brother saw that ghost around three this afternoon," Lara said.

"Well," Peck replied. "I never thought that Felipe was in this by himself. I'm hoping he'll talk and tell us who else is working with him—and where the medallion is."

"But how can you be sure Felipe did it?" Corey asked. "Maybe he was framed."

"I thought of that," Peck said. "Come with me."

The friends followed Peck into his office in the back of the precinct. The detective's desk was piled two feet high with clutter.

"I ran some routine checks on Felipe and his teammates with the Brazilian authorities," Peck said. "I'm sorry to say that Felipe has a police record as long as my left arm. I got this today—faxed to my office. If only I can find it." The gang watched as Peck dug through the heaps of papers on his desk. "I know it's here somewhere—I'm sure of it. Aha—oops, no, that's a picture of me that appeared in the newspaper after I solved the Wellington Chambers Dognapping Caper. Now where is that thing . . . ? Oh, yes. Here we go."

Peck swept the rest of the papers onto the floor and laid a photo on the table. The gang gasped. Lying there before them was a police mug shot of Felipe! It was the same unblemished face, the same shy smile. Underneath was his name: F. Luís Lopes.

Jack peered closely at the picture. "It sure looks like Felipe. But I don't know—something about him looks different. Are you sure it's really him?"

"Of course I'm sure," Detective Peck replied. "Even surer than I was when I cracked the Houston Toothpaste Spy Ring." He pointed at the picture. "This fellow is wanted in Brazil for bank robbery."

"What'll happen to him?" Sam asked.

"We'll have to send him back to Brazil for trial," Peck said. "Now I've got to get some paperwork together. You kids had better run along." With that, he shooed them back out into the hall.

Feeling depressed, Lara wandered out of the precinct and sat down on a low wall outside. Her friends joined her. "I can't believe it," Lara said. "Even though he was one of our suspects, I never would have thought Felipe was the culprit."

"No kidding," Corey said, resting her chin in her hands. "Wait until my dad finds out."

Sam looked thoughtful. "You know, nothing has been proved yet," he said suddenly. "Nothing definite, anyway."

"But they found the key," Jack pointed out.

"And the rings in the bus locker," Bryan added.

"No, Sam is right," Lara said forcefully. "That key could have been planted. I'll admit, things don't look too good for Felipe. Maybe he *is* guilty. But I won't believe that until all the facts are in."

Bryan and Jack shrugged and nodded. "I guess you're right," Jack said.

"Darn right she's right," Sam agreed. "The Brazilian team plays the Minnesota All-Stars right after we play the Hornets tonight. Let's keep our eyes and ears open."

"I'm with you guys," Corey said. "I still can't believe Felipe is guilty."

"Maybe he is, maybe he isn't," Lara said. "Either way, we've got to find out for sure!"

Pregame

After dinner with their families that evening, the five friends met again at the stadium for the big game against the Hornets. They had been hoping for weeks that the Sonics would play the Hornets for the championship.

But now they had even more things on their minds. Could they prove Felipe's innocence? Could they discover whether the ghost was real? Could they find the medallion?

"All right," Lara told her friends. "Let's

visit the Brazilian locker room and see what's cooking."

"Remember to keep your eyes open," Bryan said when they reached the locker-room door. "If Felipe is innocent, we've got to find out now." He rapped on the door three times.

No answer.

"Knock again," Lara said.

Bryan raised his hand but was interrupted by a faint "Come in."

Bryan pushed the door open. The room was empty except for Betsy, who was sitting on the bench with her head buried in her hands. Her shoulders were shaking. She looked up as the kids entered. Tears were running down her face.

"Oh, it's you kids," she said. "Isn't it awful about Felipe? I'm torn to pieces over it! To pieces, I tell you!"

She wiped her eyes with the tissue clutched in her right hand. In her left hand was the afternoon paper. On the front page was the police mug shot of Felipe.

"Wow," Sam whispered. "News travels fast."

Jack frowned thoughtfully. "I still think Felipe looks strange in that picture."

"Of course he does," Lara said. "It's a mug shot."

"It's so hard to believe," Betsy said, putting down the newspaper. "Craziness is what it is. Craziness!" With trembling fingers she began to apply another coat of orange polish to her nails. "They say he has a police record. I had no idea! How could I have known? Such a sweet man. Always smiling."

Bryan nodded. "He seemed like a good guy, that's for sure."

"Better than good," Betsy said with a sob. "And now he's in jail!"

At that moment Paulo came hobbling into the room on crutches. His foot and ankle were wrapped in layers of bandages.

"Your foot hurts a lot, huh?" Bryan asked.

"Ah, my foot—it is nothing," Paulo replied with a wave of his hand. "It's thinking about Felipe that pains me worse. I simply can't believe he would do such a thing—that he would risk the wrath of General Santiago by stealing his treasure."

Just then Sam noticed something. His heart skipped a beat. "Paulo," he said, "what happened to your hand?"

Suddenly all eyes were focused on Paulo's hands. His right finger was bandaged. The kids exchanged excited glances. Could Paulo be the thief? Could he have cut his finger climbing through the Johnstones' garage window?

Paulo shook his head. "I tell you, General Santiago is cursing me. First I sprain my ankle. Then I cut my finger."

"How'd you do that?" Jack asked.

"I had to cut some tape to wrap my ankle," Paulo explained. "But my ankle was hurting so much, I snipped the tape one too many times and cut myself by accident." He shrugged and sat down carefully on the bench beside Betsy.

The friends exchanged another glance.

Was Paulo telling the truth?

"Betsy!" an impatient voice called. "Where'd you put those extra soccer balls? We'll need them for warm-ups." The gang looked up to see Jorge stomping into the locker room. When he spotted the visitors, he frowned. "I hope you aren't giving any more of them away to these kids. I couldn't raise a cent at the fund-raiser this afternoon. It was like trying to lick water out of a slab of granite."

Betsy wiped a tear from her eye. "Jorge, you're heartless," she exclaimed. "Felipe's in jail, and all you can think about is money, money, money!"

Jorge stopped short. "Just because I'm worried about money doesn't mean I'm not also worried about Felipe, okay?"

"Do you think he really did it?" Lara asked.

"How should I know?" Jorge said. "He seems like a good and decent man, but you never know about people."

"That's right," Paulo said with a smile

as he carefully propped his foot up on a chair. "Some people even think that Jorge is a nice guy."

"Very funny," Jorge said. "Now, where are those extra soccer balls?"

"In the back where they always are," Betsy said.

Jorge scowled and stomped off toward the supply room.

"He's always unhappy about something," Paulo said as Jorge left the locker room. "He should learn to take things in stride. Look at me—I have a sprained ankle and a cut finger. But do I complain? No! Life is too short to worry."

"But you worry all the time," Betsy said. "You're the most superstitious person I've ever met."

Paulo nodded. "I worry about what is important," he said firmly. "The curse on General Santiago's medallion is worth worrying about. No, my friends, I do not fool with that curse. Some curses are fakes, but this one is very real. Trust me!"

As he and the others listened to Paulo and Betsy, Bryan suddenly noticed something—partially hidden atop one of the lockers was a soccer ball marked up with green crayon!

Bryan's heart raced. It was the soccer ball the ghost had stolen from Lara's backyard. And it was proof that there was no way Felipe could have put it there. It hadn't even been stolen until after Felipe was in jail.

Bryan decided to keep quiet about the ball for the time being. He'd wait for a moment when Betsy and Paulo weren't looking, then rip open the ball and find the medallion. Bryan couldn't hold back a grin as he envisioned the headlines in the Ridgefield papers: LOCAL BOY: HERO!

Now that, he thought to himself with a smile, *would make a great movie!*

Unfortunately, Bryan hadn't counted on Jorge's eagle eye. "Hey!" the coach barked, walking back into the room. "Give me that ball, too."

All eyes shot to the top of the locker. The rest of the kids saw the green crayon and gasped.

"Wait!" Bryan blurted out.

"Wait?" Jorge said, wheeling around. "Wait for what?"

"Uh, that's the ball you gave us yesterday," Bryan explained, sinking down onto the bench next to Betsy.

"It is? Then how'd it get back here? And what's this? Green crayon? Hey, these balls are for playing, not coloring!" The coach rubbed angrily at the green marks with his finger. "This stuff won't come off!" he huffed.

Betsy sighed and rolled her eyes. "Jorge, you've got to learn to relax. Try this." She held out a bottle of nail polish remover.

Jorge scowled but took the bottle and dabbed some of the remover on a towel.

"Now rub," Betsy said.

At the same time, Bryan heard a sound he had heard earlier that day in the supply shed: Jack sniffing.

"What are you doing?" Bryan whispered, lowering himself onto the bench next to Jack.

"Smelling," Jack replied, looking puzzled. "There's something familiar . . ." Suddenly his eyes widened.

"What?" Bryan replied. "What is it?"

"I'll tell you later," Jack whispered.

"See, Jorge? There's no problem," Betsy said, taking back the nail polish remover. "You just need to learn how to relax a little. Take me, for instance. I paint my nails. Instant relaxation! You've got to find something to do with yourself."

Jorge frowned. "Thanks for the advice," he said gruffly. He nodded to the gang. "See you on the field, guys."

The gang watched as Jorge firmly tucked the ball under his arm and left.

"Well, kids," Betsy said brightly. "It's almost time for your game to start. You'd better hustle!"

The kids realized Betsy was right. It was twenty after seven—game time was in ten minutes. Mr. Lester and the rest of the team would be wondering where they were. Besides, the rest of the Brazilian team would be coming in soon to change for their game. There was nothing more the kids could do here—at least, not for now.

As soon as they were outside, Jack turned to his friends excitedly. "That smell!" he exclaimed. "Remember how I smelled something weird in the shed?"

"I remember," Sam said. "I didn't smell a thing—you must have some kind of supersonic nose."

Jack grinned. "You bet I do," he declared. "And my supersonic nose sniffed out a major clue. I finally figured out in the locker room what that smell was—nail polish remover!"

Lara gasped. "Nail polish remover? That points to Betsy."

"Betsy?" Corey repeated. "You mean she was the one who ripped up those balls?"

"Well, they keep all sorts of things in the supply shed. Someone could have been using turpentine earlier. After all, she seemed pretty upset about Felipe," Sam said.

"And I still think Paulo might be the culprit," Lara said thoughtfully as the kids walked toward the field.

"Just what I was thinking," Jack said. "He could be faking that ankle injury. We all saw he had a Band-Aid on his finger and everything."

"Then Paulo's our man!" Bryan said.

Lara sighed. "Well, maybe we're jumping the gun. We have lots of evidence, but none of it positively proves anything—yet. Let's keep our eyes open during the game."

"If there are any more clues, I'll sniff 'em out," Jack said.

"And after you run around for a while, I'll be trying *not* to sniff you," Bryan joked. "Come on! It's almost game time!"

HERE COME THE HORNETS

"Thank goodness you made it," Mr. Lester called as the gang ran onto the field. "Statistically speaking, soccer teams don't generally win when playing with only six players."

"Sorry we're late," Lara called. "We got delayed."

"It's okay," Mr. Lester replied. "Though you missed my pep talk on the history of the adding machine."

As the team took their positions and began to warm up, the PA system crackled to life. "Here it is," the announcer cried. "The match you've been waiting for! A special night game for one of the county's fiercest rivalries—the Smithfield Sonics versus the Johnsonville Hornets!"

Bryan looked around in awe. He really felt like a character in a movie. The stadium was jam-packed with cheering fans. It was already dark, but the bright lights lit up the field dramatically. He took a deep breath and did a few stretches, trying to concentrate on the task ahead of him.

Meanwhile, across the field, Corey was looking over the other team. Standing across from her was George, a large, dark-haired boy.

"Ready to get destroyed?" George asked with a smile.

"I wouldn't even know how to get destroyed," Corey replied with a grin.

"Well, you're about to learn!" George said. He punched Corey playfully on the shoulder. Even though the two teams were rivals, some of them were friends.

Finally it was time for the game to start. The referee blew a whistle and placed the ball at midfield. Corey took a final look over her opponents. To her right was Randy Miles, a boy with a fake tattoo of a pirate ship on his right biceps. To her left was Elmore Gritch, a tall boy with blond hair. Corey knew he was one of the fastest runners in the county. On the sidelines stood the Hornet coach, Mr. Anderchuk.

"Take it to them, team," he called to his players. "Be aggressive out there!"

Corey glanced at the stands behind the coach. It seemed as though everyone in the county was there to watch the game. She smiled. This was it—the finals!

Another whistle blew. Instantly forgetting about the crowd, Corey moved on the ball. She passed it off to Jack, who quickly tapped it back to Lara at half-back.

The Hornets scrambled to keep up, but the Sonics controlled the flow early.

"Cover them!" Mr. Anderchuk screamed from the sidelines. "Come on, team!"

Corey was proving especially difficult for the Hornets to cover. She wanted to make up for that afternoon's game, when Ricky Harling had stuck to her like glue. This time Corey was determined to roam and score. Every time George caught up with her, she managed to slip away from him again.

"Can't keep up?" she asked George, who was already winded, after a few minutes of play.

"I'm with you, Corey," George replied gamely.

Corey cut to her left. George tried to follow, but slipped. Seeing the opening, Jack passed Corey the ball. Corey dribbled left, then chipped a pass to Lara. Lara controlled the ball with her chest, gave a slight head fake and shook a defender, and passed the ball back to Corey.

With a quick burst of speed, Corey suddenly had a clear shot on goal. She cocked her leg, dribbled, and faked left. The goalie leaned that way. In a flash, Corey passed the ball to Jack.

Boom! The ball thundered into the right side of the goal.

"Yes!" Jack cried, pumping his fists. He ran over to Corey and threw his arms around her. "Nice setup!"

The crowd cheered wildly. Mr. Lester jumped up and down while simultaneously punching numbers into his calculator.

"Victory is practically ensured," he cried. "According to my analysis, only one junior team has ever lost a championship after scoring the first goal within two minutes of play."

On the other side of the field, Mr. Anderchuk paced the sidelines, calling instructions to his team. "Defense, team! Defense! Hold them back."

"All right, players," the ref called. "The clock's running here. No pun intended, but let's keep things rolling."

Lara congratulated Jack and Corey, then jogged back to her position. She was thrilled by the goal, but somehow she couldn't keep her mind on the game. As excited as she was to be playing in the finals against the Hornets, she kept thinking about the missing medallion. Was Felipe really guilty? The police thought so. Was Betsy in on it? Jack's nose thought so. Then there was the cut on Paulo's finger. . . .

"Hey! Watch it!"

Lara looked up to see the ball flying toward her head. Just in time she took a step back and managed to deflect the ball downfield to a teammate.

"Way to keep your head in the game," Jack called, running by her after the ball.

Lara shot Jack a glance and tore downfield after him.

I've got to concentrate on the game! she told herself.

But Lara couldn't shake her gut feeling that Felipe was innocent. She knew from the hundreds of mysteries she had read that gut feelings weren't always reliable, but something told her that hers was right. And she couldn't stop thinking about it.

Toward the end of the first half, Lara saw something that almost made her forget the game entirely. Walking into the stadium, followed by three uniformed police officers, was Detective Peck, complete with trench coat.

Maybe Felipe talked, Lara thought anxiously. *Maybe they're here to make some arrests.*

Then she saw two other people she wasn't expecting to see—Betsy and Paulo. Betsy was helping Paulo maneuver into the first row with his crutches. When the two Brazilians saw Lara looking at them, they waved and cheered.

Wow, Lara thought, waving back. *If they're guilty, they sure aren't acting like it!*

Lara's heart was pounding now, and not from the exertion of the game. Her mind was reeling with clues and ideas. She thought it all through from the beginning: the missing medallion, the police search, the break-in at Corey's garage. . . . Lara smiled when she remembered Mr. Johnstone's precious new car. He had nearly died when he found that smudge mark. . . .

That *orange* smudge mark!

Lara gasped. Could the smudge on the car have been from Betsy's orange nail polish?

Just then the buzzer sounded to end the first half. The score was still 1–0.

Lara rushed to the sidelines, dying to tell her friends what she had figured out. But the minute she reached the bench, Mr. Lester launched into a vigorous pep talk.

"Never in my coaching days have I had a player who shoots the ball with such accuracy as Corey!" the accountant announced. "It reminds me of a story. Once upon a time, a lawyer and a dentist went bowling together. Now . . ."

"Pssst . . ." someone hissed.

Lara looked over. It was Jack. Corey, Sam, and Bryan looked over, too.

"Have any of you figured anything else out?" Jack said quietly.

"I think so," Lara whispered.

". . . and so the dentist took careful aim and rolled a strike . . ." Mr. Lester went on.

Quickly Lara filled her friends in on her orange smudge theory.

"It also fits that I smelled nail polish remover in the shed," Jack said.

"So Betsy *is* the one," Bryan said. "And if Paulo was faking his ankle injury, it would be the perfect alibi for an accomplice."

"They have to be the ones," Lara said. "And I think it's about time we had a word with them." She glanced over at the stands. They were gone!

But before she could utter another word, all the lights in the stadium went out, plunging the field into total darkness.

BLACKOUT

The entire stadium was pitch-dark.

"I can't see a thing," Sam called.

"Just stay cool," Corey cried.

"Don't hurt yourselves, team!" Mr. Lester exclaimed.

Suddenly, Lara felt a shape rush past her, heading toward the field.

Was it a ghost? A thief? Everyone was talking at once, pushing, shoving, grabbing.

Lara's eyes were beginning to adjust to the darkness. She could make out the dim outlines of her four friends. Before anyone could say a word, there was a cry from the other side of the field.

"Help! A ghost!"

"Let's go!" Lara yelled, running onto the dark field.

"Let's go?" Bryan said. "You've got to be crazy. There's a ghost out there!"

"Yeah," Lara said. "A ghost who may be looking for a medallion!"

But Lara wasn't the only one bursting onto the field. Detective Peck and three uniformed officers, equipped with flashlights, were also combing the grounds.

"Watch it, kids," Peck called as he rushed toward the running shape. "We'll handle this!"

But the gang kept coming. They hadn't spent all day trying to crack the case to be left out at the moment of capture!

Then another terrified voice pierced the air.

"There's another ghost!"

"No, it's the same one!"

Two ghosts? Lara thought with a start.

"This is crazy," Sam said to Jack. "Two ghosts? I can't see an inch in front of my face."

Peck's flashlight beam fixed on a shape moving on the other side of the field. Then one of his officers shined her flashlight on another shape! There *were* two ghosts!

"After him!" Jack called, charging recklessly into the dark.

"Careful," Bryan called. "It could be dangerous!"

"Danger is my middle name!" Jack yelled back.

Bryan turned and ran to the left, hoping to head off the white figure. As he drew closer, he saw that the ghost was carrying something. "I think he has the soccer ball," Bryan yelled to his friends.

The figure kept running, still pursued by five kids and four police officers.

Bryan couldn't see where he was going. He kept his eyes trained on the white figure—which turned out to be a mistake. Bryan's legs got tangled up with a soccer ball and he pitched over onto his face. "Ow!" he cried, grabbing the ball.

Before he could stand up, he heard Detective Peck's voice.

"Stop!"

The ghost had doubled back and was galloping straight toward Bryan.

Without thinking, Bryan rolled the soccer ball as hard as he could across the grass. It hooked sharply left and hit the phantom in the legs.

"Umpf!" The ghost hit the dirt with a loud thud, and the ball he was carrying slipped out of his grasp. Seconds later, Peck was there slapping on handcuffs.

Suddenly, out of the darkness came the other ghost. He ran straight into Detective Peck. The detective went flying, and the ghost kept on running.

Corey stuck her leg out. The ghost tripped and sprawled out onto the grass just as the stadium lights came back on!

The gang blinked. Lara looked around. Two figures in skeleton outfits were lying on the ground. The crowd was on its feet, watching the action on the field. And there by the exit was—Betsy!

"Detective Peck!" Lara cried. "Go get her! She's in on it!"

Peck looked where Lara was pointing. "You sure, kid?"

"Yes! I'll explain later!"

Peck motioned to one of the officers, who took off like a shot in Betsy's direction.

Meanwhile, it was time to unmask the two ghosts. Peck walked over to the second skeleton and lifted up the mask.

"It's Wayne!" Jack cried.

"You mean you went to all this trouble to scare us?" Corey asked in disbelief.

The boy just looked at the ground. "Just thought I'd have a little fun and scare you kids a little . . ." he mumbled.

"We'll see what your parents have to say about this, young man," Detective

Peck scolded. "Why, I could lock you up for obstructing justice. Were you in on this alone, son?"

"Gus was the voice on the PA this afternoon, and he turned off the lights just now," Wayne admitted. He looked close to tears.

"That's a pretty low trick, even for you guys," Bryan said.

"Well, that's part of the mystery solved, but who is the other ghost?" Jack asked.

In one motion the detective lifted the mask off the handcuffed skeleton.

"Good God!" the detective exclaimed. "I thought I had you in custody already!"

The man, who looked exactly like Felipe, gave the detective a hard glare. "You wish!" he snapped.

"I think I can explain, Detective Peck," Jack said calmly. "I knew there was something funny about Felipe's mug shot. Felipe has a mole on his cheek. The guy in the mug shot and our ghost here don't. You arrested the wrong man, sir."

"Then who is he?" Detective Peck exclaimed in shock.

"I'm Felipe's brother, Luís. You haven't got anything against me without the medallion as evidence."

"I think we can help with that, too, Detective," Lara said. "Could we see his hands?"

Peck wrinkled his brow. "His hands? Why in the world . . . ?"

"Please, sir. . . ."

Peck sighed, but he checked the prisoner's hands. Sure enough, the twin had cuts on his palm and right index finger.

Once that was confirmed, Bryan pointed at the soccer ball that had tripped the ghost. "And if that's not enough to link him to the break-in at the Johnstones' and vandalizing the soccer balls in the supply shed," he said, "I think you'll find the medallion in there."

Now Peck was really surprised. "What? How do you know?"

Bryan glanced at his friends. "Well,

when I knocked down the ghost with the ball, my eyes were adjusted to the dark enough to see that it hooked."

"So?" Jack asked.

"Well, don't you remember when we first got the ball? It hooked then, too. I think the medallion has thrown off the ball's balance." He placed the ball on the ground and kicked it to Sam. It went straight for about five feet and then sharply veered left.

Bryan beamed triumphantly.

"All right. Let's get to the bottom of this!" Peck declared. After a few moments of searching, he located a knife in the pocket of his trench coat. Then, with a few hard cuts along the seams, he split the ball open. Bryan reached inside, fished around for a second—and pulled out a gold medallion with an engraving of a warrior on horseback.

"Wow!" Jack said. "The missing medallion!"

Peck held the medallion above his

head. “General Santiago’s medallion has been recovered!” he announced.

The crowd applauded long and loud. The five friends gave each other high fives.

“All right, you,” Peck said to Felipe’s twin. “Off to the station house.” Peck read the prisoner his rights and began to escort him off the field.

Just then Mr. Lester came hustling onto the field. “We’ve still got a game to finish here. Second half, remember? Let’s keep our lead. It’s one to nothing—and the Hornets want blood!”

A Game to Remember

"That halftime show was brought to you from the Ridgefield County Police Department," the announcer joked over the PA. "But now let's return to the game!"

The two teams hurried back to the field.

"Okay," the ref called. "Second half. Let's get started. Hornets will throw in the ball at midfield."

"All right!" Bryan yelled from the goal. "Let's make like a ghost and stop them dead!"

Sam smirked. "Pretty bad, Bryan."

Bryan grinned. "I know, but we've got this game in the bag. I can afford to make a rotten joke."

But Bryan had spoken too soon. While the Sonics were chasing ghosts, the Hornets had actually taken time to come up with a new game plan. Mr. Anderchuk had decided to move an extra player back on defense to deal with Corey.

"Get ready to be haunted by me this half," George told Corey at midfield.

"No way," Corey said. "I've had enough haunting for one day."

The buzzer sounded and a Hornet inbounded the ball to George, who dribbled down the right wing, then centered the ball to Randy Miles. Randy trapped the ball and quickly passed to Elmore Gritch out on the left wing. Elmore raced downfield, and as he drew Lara and Sam off their men to cover him, lofted a beautiful cross to George right in front of the goal. Bryan dove just as George got a foot on the ball.

“Save!” the announcer yelled.

Play after play, the Hornets dominated the second half, but with ten minutes left to play, they still hadn’t managed to put the ball into the net. Bryan allowed himself a small grin.

Up one to nothing. This game is over! he thought to himself.

He was already back in his thoughts of limos and his speech to accept the key to the city when Elmore Gritch broke free at midfield on a fast break. As Elmore entered the goalie box, Bryan stepped away from the net to cut off his shot. Elmore made a slight move to the left, and Bryan threw himself at the ball. But he committed too soon! Elmore cut back to the right and dribbled straight to the open net. Bryan could only watch from the ground as Elmore gently pushed the ball into the goal with his instep.

“Goal!” the ref called.

“Hang in there,” Mr. Lester called from the sidelines.

"Tough play, Bryan," Lara said, helping him off the ground. "There wasn't anything you could have done."

"I guess not," Bryan answered dejectedly.

Sam trotted over and dusted off Bryan's back. "Don't worry, pal, we'll pull out of this."

But the Sonics simply couldn't penetrate the Hornets' defense. Every time Corey or Jack went for the ball, someone was on them like glue. The seemingly endless supply of energy they had had in the first half had somehow disappeared.

Finally, with less than five minutes to go, Corey intercepted a long cross-field pass from one Hornet to another. But instead of waiting for the rest of the Sonics to get back on defense and trying to set up a play, she sprinted for the goal. By the time the Hornets chased her down the field, it was too late. She drew the goalie out of position and chipped a shot just over his head. Before he could scramble back, the ball bounced once and into the net.

"Goal!" exclaimed the announcer. "The score is now two–one, Sonics!"

"That was beautiful, Corey!" Jack cried, running over. "That should be the nail in the coffin."

"Thanks," Corey huffed. She was exhausted, but knew there were only about three minutes left to play.

Corey was grateful when Mr. Lester wisely shifted her and some players back on defense, quoting a ream of statistics to support his decision. The Sonics were just fighting to hold their lead.

At the same time, the Hornets were playing for their lives, determined to score and tie things up. Corey knew that if the game went into sudden death, the fresher and less tired Hornets would have the advantage.

Shot after shot thundered toward the Sonics' goal.

Kick!

Save!

Kick!

Wide to the left.

A rebound . . . a header . . .

SAVE!

The crowd was cheering wildly. "What a goalie!" "Go, Sonics!"

"Come on, Hornets!" Mr. Anderchuk cried. "Let's tie it up again!"

With thirty seconds remaining, George took a hard, low shot from just inside the goalie box. Sam dove to head it out-of-bounds, but as he reached out to brace his fall, he knocked the ball out of the way with his hands instead.

The sound of the whistle made Bryan's blood run cold.

"Penalty kick," the ref called.

"Oh, no!" Sam cried.

"Let George take it," Mr. Anderchuk called.

It was one-on-one now—George against Bryan with everything on the line. George took some advice from his teammates and coach, then got ready to kick.

Bryan crouched low, ready to leap in any direction. He tried to block out the noise from the crowd. He had to concentrate. Stopping a penalty kick was largely a matter of guessing which way the opponent would go. Would George try for the right or left side of the goal? Bryan couldn't tell. George was left-footed. Would that make a difference? Had George kicked to one side of the goal more than the other? Bryan didn't think so.

In any case, there wasn't any more time to think about it. George was trotting up the field, his eye on the ball. His leg was snapping back.

Boom!

Bryan dove to his right as the crowd rose to its feet.

He had guessed correctly!

The ball rocketed toward the corner of the goal. Bryan stretched his hands . . . if he could only reach it . . . he stretched out his fingers—and felt the ball bounce off them.

The ball deflected to the left—but would it go in, anyway? Before he could see, Bryan landed heavily, facedown on the ground.

Bryan lay flat in the grass and listened to the crowd cheer. He didn't dare lift his head. Had the Hornets scored?

Oh, no! he thought. *Not again! This time it went in! It had to!*

But Bryan didn't have to keep guessing for long.

"You did it!" Sam shouted, running over.

"Great save!" Mr. Lester called from the sidelines.

Slowly it sunk in. *No goal!* The buzzer sounded. The Sonics had won!

Bryan was mobbed.

Jack pounded him on the back. "Unbelievable, Bryan!"

"That was incredible!" Lara cried.

"A great end to a great day!" Corey said, slapping Sam's outstretched hand.

"You said it," Jack replied with a grin. "Can you believe we captured a crook—"

"You mean a ghost," Corey interrupted.

"Okay, can you believe we captured a *ghost*," Jack said, "*and* a championship, all in the same day!"

"Hey, check it out," Sam said excitedly, pointing to the stands.

"Felipe!" Corey shouted. The gang raced over to the stands.

"Felipe?" Lara called. "Is that you?"

The young man smiled. "That's right. They let me out of jail—thanks to you!"

"Hey, it was our pleasure," Jack said.

Felipe grinned, then quickly filled them in on what had happened. "You see," he said, "I knew all along that my brother was the one in trouble."

"Why didn't you tell the police?" Jack asked.

Felipe sighed. "I couldn't bear to see him go back to jail. I thought maybe they wouldn't find enough evidence and they'd have to let me go."

"But, Felipe," Lara said, "you ran the risk of being convicted of a crime you didn't commit. You could have gone to jail for years!"

Felipe shrugged. "I suppose that's true. But what can I say? Luís wasn't always such a bad person." He sighed again. "And he is my brother."

"Felipe," Lara asked. "Do you know if they caught Betsy?"

Felipe nodded. "They got her, all right." He looked sad. "Such a nice person. I don't know what she was doing smuggling a stolen medallion."

"Maybe she wanted to meet some ghosts," Bryan said.

"More likely she wanted a barrelful of money," Sam said.

"That's right!"

Everyone looked up. Detective Peck was walking over.

"We got a full confession, kids. Turns out that Betsy and Luís were part of a major South American smuggling ring. They had about twenty-four hours to get the medallion to an eccentric millionaire in Canada."

"Wow!" Lara said. "So that's why they needed the ball back so quickly after they gave it to us."

"Right," Peck said. "Now, let's see . . . I have it written down right here." The detective fiddled through his trench coat and finally produced a crinkled piece of yellow paper. "Ah, yes! Betsy gave you the ball as a gift to get it out of the locker room, but then needed it back immediately—sooner than she expected. That's why she and Luís broke into Corey's garage last night. And after seeing Gus and Wayne pull that stunt with the ghost of General Santiago, they decided it was the perfect way to scare people off the trail and recover the medallion while disguised. By the time we put things together and figured out that Felipe had been set up, Luís and Betsy planned to be miles away.

"Luís managed to track the ball to Lara's house and grab it from her yard. But then Jorge unwittingly took the ball back and put it with all the others. The thieves had to try the ghost trick again during the final game to finally recover the medallion."

Sam nodded thoughtfully. "That explains something else. During our game this afternoon Bryan and I saw—or thought we saw—Felipe in the stadium. Bryan yelled hello, but he didn't even answer."

"It wasn't me," Felipe said. "It must have been my brother. I guess he was getting ready for his first performance as the ghost of General Santiago."

"Wow," Bryan said. "And I thought I was being ignored."

Felipe grinned. "I would never ignore the star goalie."

"Aw, well," Bryan said modestly. "'Star' is such a strong word. Sure I made a few stunning saves. You might even say that I won the game for—"

"Hey!" Lara interrupted. "I just thought of something else." She shook her head. "I'm such an idiot!"

She turned to Paulo, who was sitting nearby, his swollen ankle propped up.

"We owe you an apology," Lara told him.

"Me?" Paulo laughed. "What for?"

"Well, we suspected you had been faking and that you were working with Betsy. I mean, you do have a cut finger. But I just realized that there's no way you could have broken into a garage by climbing through Corey's garage window with that ankle."

Paulo nodded. "That's true. But don't feel so bad." He grinned. "I *could* have been faking."

The kids laughed. Just then the Brazilian team charged onto the field, as Jorge cheered them on loudly from the sidelines.

"I guess Jorge is innocent, too," Jack said.

"He had a solid alibi the whole time," Peck stated. "While your three soccer balls were being ripped open this afternoon, he was at that fund-raiser."

The gang nodded and exchanged glances. "I guess we forgot about that," Lara admitted.

"Pretty funny," Corey said. "He didn't even want to go to that fund-raiser—but it proves he's innocent."

"Right," Peck said. "Anyway, kids, thanks for your help. We've got the medallion back, and we've got our suspects in jail." Peck shook their hands all around. "I wouldn't be surprised if you all turned out to be great detectives—like me—someday." With that, he turned and hurried away.

"Well," Jack said with a sigh. "I'm kind of sad it's all over. What should we do now?"

"I know what I'm doing," Bryan said. "There's a game to watch! Brazil against the Minnesota All-Stars."

The gang looked toward the field just as one of the Brazilian players rocketed a ball into the goal.

"Bryan," Jack said, "you are a genius!"